For Ian Wilcock, not least for his rascally cuisine - J.W.

For Luke, the Lion of Twickenham - K.P.

First published in Great Britain in 1994 by Andersen Press Ltd.,
20 Vauxhall Bridge Road, London SW1V 2SA.
This paperback edition first published in 2009 by Andersen Press Ltd.
Published in Australia by Random House Australia Pty.,
Level 3, 100 Pacific Highway, North Sydney, NSW 2060.
Text copyright © Jeanne Willis, 1994.
Illustration copyright © Korky Paul, 1994.

Colour separated in Switzerland by Photolitho AG, Zürich.
Printed and bound in Singapore by Tien Wah Press Pte Ltd.

10   9   8   7   6   5   4   3   2   1

British Library Cataloguing in Publication Data available.

ISBN 978 1 84270 717 3

This book has been printed on acid-free paper

Zebra drawing on previous page by Zoë Paul aged 5 years.

THE RASCALLY CAKE

Jeanne Willis
Korky Paul

Andersen Press

Mr Rufus Skumskins O'Parsley
Wouldn't eat supper unless it was ghastly.
Wormcast butties, tubes of glue,
Pans of slugs in slimy stew,
Bogey burgers, brown rat roast,
Fat black tadpoles squashed on toast,
Washed down with a cup of string.
Can you imagine such a thing?

One morning Rufus woke in bed,
Picked up a pen and scratched his head,
"I know," he said, "I think I'll make
An extra special Christmas cake."

He smiled and smacked his lips with greed
And scribbled down the things he'd need.
Ten pounds of flour, six rotten eggs,
One hundred hairy spiders' legs,
Some muck, some moths, some mouldy leaves
And several snotty handkerchiefs,
A jug of spit, some garden snails,
The clippings from his fingernails.

He wrote out fifty pages' worth
Of filthy things he could unearth,
And then he wrote the recipe.
How ghastly could O'Parsley be?
Far ghastlier, for up he got
And rustled up a cooking pot -
A reeking, rusty rubbish bin.
(What else could he put that lot in?)
Having done that, off he went
To find the foul ingredients.

Two days later he came back
And grinning like a maniac,
Put on his apron and his hat
And heated up the cooking fat.
In went a tramp's sock! In went the fleas!
In went the scabs from a schoolboy's knees!
In went a cowpat! In went mud!
In went blubber, the bones and the blood!

Soon the pot could hold no more,
Horrible blobs bubbled onto the floor,
It dribbled and wibbled and
spurted and popped,
It wobbled and spluttered and
splattered and slopped,
It coughed and it burped and it tumbled about

And to Rufus's horror,

began to climb out.

"Whoops!" exclaimed Rufus, "I've made a mistake,
Something's gone terribly wrong with this cake.
I've used too much flour . . . the fat was too hot."
Off flew the dustbin lid! Out the cake got!

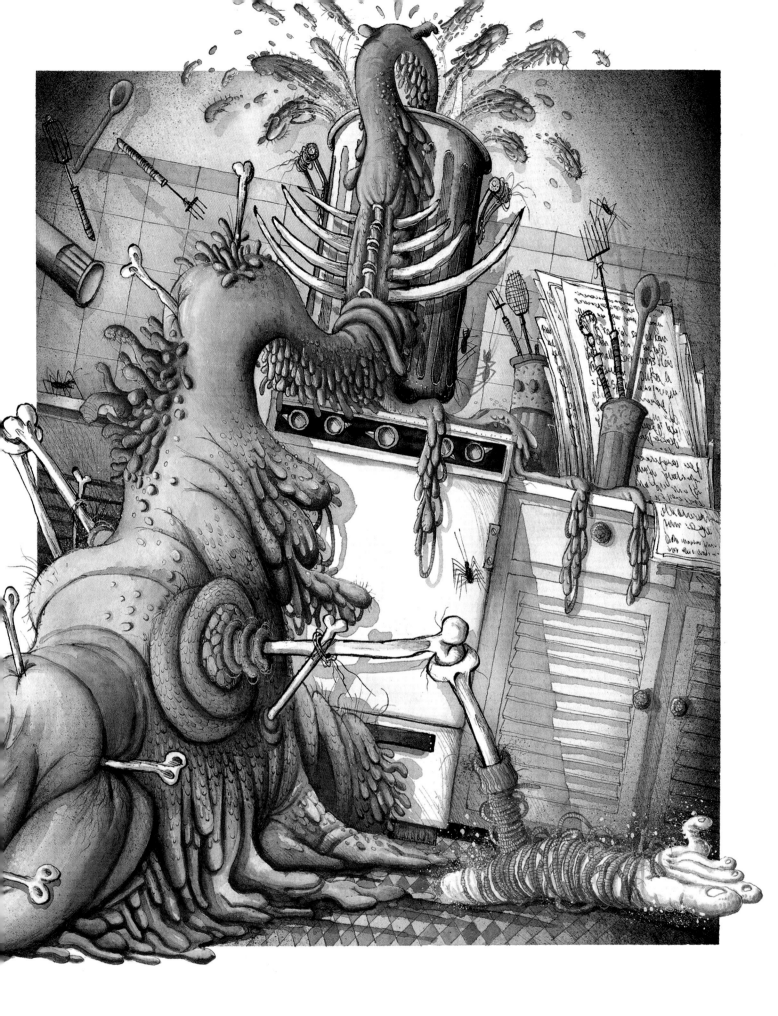

It started to chase him 'round cupboards and chairs,
Then into the hallway and straight up the stairs.
"Help!" cried O'Parsley, then, "What have I done?"
Hotly pursued by the man-eating bun,
He ran to the bedroom and locked the door tight
And hid in the wardrobe and shivered with fright.

Under the gap between carpet and door
The rascally cake mixture started to pour.
With long, spongey fingers and lardy white toes
It searched and it sniffed with its drippy green nose.
"I've got you!" it gurgled and gave him a tweak,
"And now I shall eat you! Keep still and don't squeak."

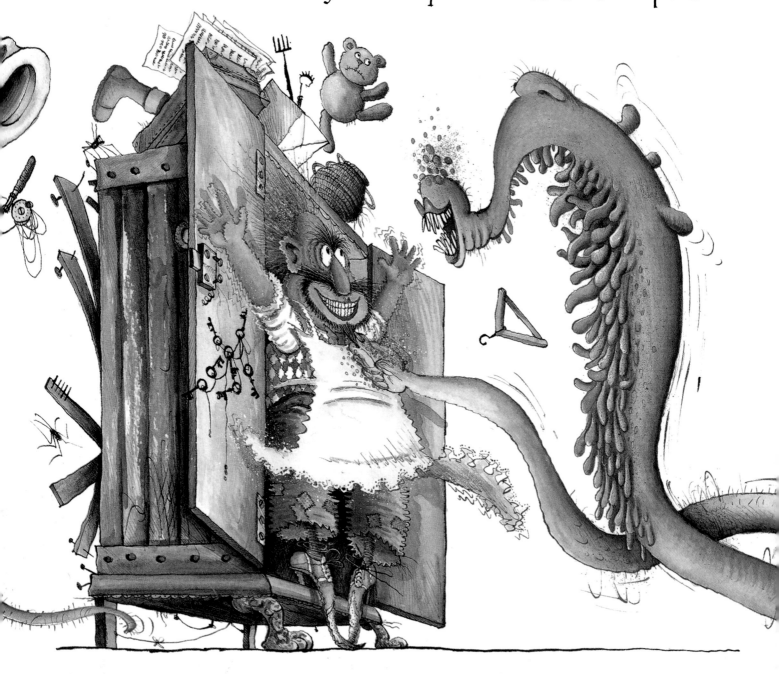

Please do not worry for Rufus's sake,
Your sympathy really should lie with the cake,
For the cake took one mouthful of Rufus and said,
"Revolting! Disgusting! I'm poisoned!" and fled.

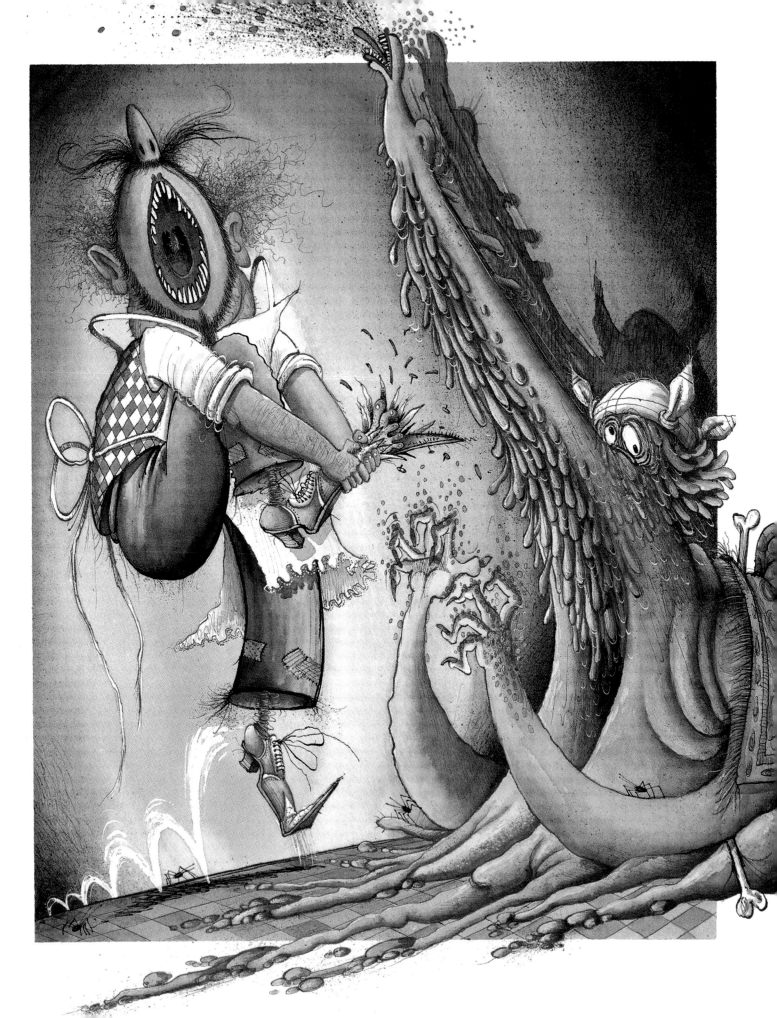

Where did it go to? Well, nobody knows,
The rats wouldn't eat it
and nor would the crows.
According to Rufus, it wanders at large,
Stinking of rubbish and rancid old marg.

Mr O'Parsley decided to change;
He doesn't eat anything smelly or strange,
Just cucumber sandwiches, lettuce and ham,
Thinly sliced bread with a spoonful of jam,
A lightly-boiled egg, the occasional steak,
But never, oh, NEVER does Rufus eat . . . CAKE!!!!

More Andersen Press picture books for you to enjoy:

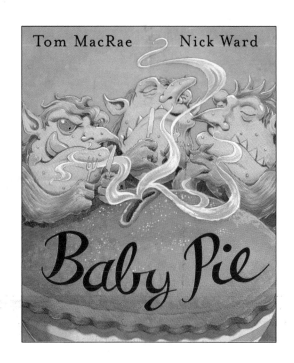

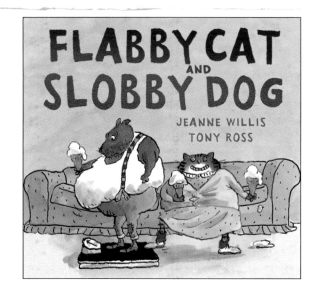

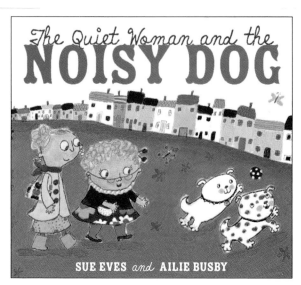